THE STORY OF A WARRIOR

PAR-1

TEJRUDRA DHANKAR

Contents

Contents

Preface

Hi everyone there! I am Tejrudra Dhankar. My book "The Story Of A Warrior" is a novella, that tells us the story of Tyler Stark. Tyler Stark of Raisens, the book does not entirely tell the story but also comes up with the challenges that one faces while growing. The story is suitable for any age. If you are empathetic and considerate of others, you may relate to the character. It took me more than 2 years to complete the story.

This story would help you cope with things better.

Looking forward to make you all feel good.

Hope you all enjoy reading it.

Prologue

Psst . . . . It is me, the warrior of Raisens. Ohhhhh! My bad, you probably don't know me. This book is written by me to tell my people and warriors my story. A story of a warrior who fought to get recognition, to get support, to get love, to get someone's heart, and many more things. The place where I used to live was situated in the Raisens Empire, the 'Capital City of Raisens'. You probably not have heard of me. Therefore, I would start from the start.

CHAPTER ONE

THE BEGINNING

I was a warrior. Warriors are some of the people who fight and guard their respective nations. In total, there are 7 great nations and 2 nations. The empire in which I lived, is one of the best nations- The Raisens. When I was 15 I was given my first mission to complete. When I turned 11, I joined the warrior's school to get myself transformed into a powerful man.

There were two other reasons, which invigorated me with the courage, to join a place where......................... The first reason was that I was an orphan. Nobody believed in me because of this so all I wished was to get myself happy. Nobody knew who my parents were and where I came from.

Then, there was a couple who took care of me, since when I was an infant.

However, it was also an illusion because when I turned five both of them died because of some medical issues. I was too little to know what it meant to lose someone.

They were my parents, and I was their son. At least they treated me with all of their love and care. I still remember the smile of my mom and dad when I learned to walk. Although they were not my real parents they never showed any kind of abhorrence towards me. They were merchants who lived in a well-made house. When I was five, their illness became severe. They knew I would have to live a miserable life without them, but it cannot be helped.

I still remember it, it was a showery twilight, I was not getting to my bed, and all my mom asked me was to sleep quickly.

However, I Was a very vile kid, I just shamelessly told her to read me a story She kept refusing but I didn't agree with it and kept my opinion over hers. She started to read for me, "My son should become a king shortly to make me the queen of the empire so that I could find a princess for him. The story says my son, long time back when the great moraine, who marched towards Raisens with his military of over 200,000 warriors, there was lord seventh in his way defending the Raisens and Elfins with only 100,000 warriors."

All of a sudden, my mom became silent. Her hand which she had tightly held my hand near my chest loosened.

I kept asking her what happened next but I was too naive to understand that she had already left me alone and gone to heaven. I got myself up to find my dad, to ask him what happened to my mom. I kept searching for him in every corner of the house and shouted, "Dad, Dad.....................".

I was in tears and finally found my dad in his room lying in his bed. I asked him for help sobbingly but after some time, I realized that they would no longer come for my help.

The moment I realized this I ran towards my mom held his hands tightly near my chest and slept as she asked me to. Both of the stars left me that night. The next morning the doctor came to the home next morning and saw me *sleeping with my mom and murmured to himself, "What a love of mom and son."*

But the reality was the whole night I wasn't able to sleep. Because my face was filled with tears. That was the first day I felt a sharp pain in my chest. Probably it was because of............... After this when he came close he realized that my mom had died and I was crying holding her hand.

The doctor said in shock, "OH! God!" he hurriedly ran to get help. My parents were friends with the King Ninth. That morning the king himself came to witness the death of his dearest friend and my beloved parents.

CHAPTER TWO

THE KING'S DECISION

My parent's funeral was held on the 3rd day after their demise. My parents who were the most fabulous, died. My father Mr. Stark owned a large field and some precious stones. After him, I was the one who inherited these things. I also inherited something from my mom, she always said to me, "My dear, be a heroic warrior and be the one to unleash the best abilities a warrior can have."

***

Every warrior unleashes many abilities after he turns 11. Only the ones who can unleash them are capable of being warriors.

Some of the major abilities that are unleashed by the people of Raisens are:

1.

   Fire resistivity

As the name suggests the wielder of this ability, has resistance to fire. He can stay in fire and can fight for himself for around 30 minutes. After this, his fire gets extinguished automatically.

1.

   Power users

They have high raw strength in their arms. Because of this reason, they use heavy swords or hammers to crush the heads of their enemies.

3.

   Water breathers

They can live in the water for at least 30 minutes with ease. They can even extract the water from the ground by focusing on the water molecules which are beneath them.

4.

Healers

They can heal themselves as well as others. Healers can heal others more efficiently and faster than they can themselves.

5.

Watcher

They can sense the presence of Raisens, Elfins, humans, etc.

We have other abilities with us as well but these are some of the common. For example, we had sorceresses, and witches with us as well.

***

The King Jon decided to take me to his place. He thought I would feel better if

was under his jurisdiction. And in that sense, it was better for me as well. I got someone who liked to look after me, the king the queen, and their daughter Ellena.

She was a year older than I was. She always cared for me and treated me with her love. King Jon and Lady Jenny let me share a room with their daughter. We both shared the same path and dream, a dream to become a fine warrior and after that to be the next supreme leader of Raisens. Actually whenever I used to go out to play every kid of our age made fun of me.

Because of the death of Mr. And Mrs. Stark. However, I got dear Ellena by my side and to rescue me from those terrible laughs. She always showed love for me. We stayed together, ate together, and lived together under the same roof.

CHAPTER THREE

THE LORD ELVIN OF THE ELFINS

King Jon and lord Elvin of the Elfins had been friends for about 30 years. Lord Elvin was an elf was the supreme leader of Elfins. I still remember in the year 991 A.G. Lord Elvin came to our land to see his dearest friend.

***

(Year 991, at the Elvin palace)

"My lord, we are good to go towards the Raisens with 500 warriors, we have taken precious stones and jewels for the lady of Raisens," said Joffrey to lord Elvin.

"Good to know all this, we must depart from here at noon so that it takes us 5 long days to reach the landing" told lord Elvin to Joffrey.

Joffrey got silent and did not respond to the lord. Nevertheless, the king saw through his silence and asked if there was any bad news. "My lord the reason for my silence is, Mr. Stark and Mrs. Stark have passed away," Said Joffrey who was filled with melancholy.

This made the king dejected.

When he was younger, Mr. Stark, King Jon, and lord Elvin used to play together whenever lord Elvin came to Raisens with his father.

***

Lord Elvin was a 50-year-old elf. However, his looks made him look no more than 20 years at that age. Lord Elvin when arrived at our place, the king and queen both got themselves up to get him in our home.

Ellena and I were both in the field helping the farmers count the corn. Someone from the chateau came to take both of us to the palace.

We were overjoyed after listening to this because it was unusual for us to be called by the king. When we reached our house, we were asked by the queen to behave properly.

Queen took us both to prepare us. She ordered both of us violently, "If you don't behave properly, I am going to throw you both in front of the griffin that our king rides." Ellena fearlessly answered, "Mom do you think this will make us fear you" After completing this looked at me. She must have expected me to agree with her. But all I said was, "Ellena, I don't know what a griffin looks like."

Her mom smiled a little and said politely, "You are too good and kind to be with my daughter, she is going to make you a fearless warrior."

CHAPTER FOUR

THE FOREST OF FANTASY!!!

Queen Jenny was a generous and ecstatic woman. She was able to see through anybody's heart. She could tell what lies inside a person's mind and heart. She took us to our room and took off our clothes. She gave both Ellena and me new clothes. The new clothes, which we got, were opulent.

***

(Description of Lady Jenny)

She was around 30 years old, with long golden hair that cascaded down her back in soft waves. Her eyes were also a striking golden hue, shining like the sun. She stood tall at 5 feet and 8 inches, with a graceful posture and an effortless confidence that added to her allure. She was one the most beautiful women in Raisens. He was exceptionally better than any other woman of her age. She was bestowed with a character that everybody dreams of.

Her golden eyes could see through the person and could reveal the true feelings of that person.

***

A worker at the palace knocked on our room and asked permission to enter into the room. Queen Jenny refused and asked the purpose of his coming. The worker told us that the king and lord Elvin wished to see us both. Lady ordered the worker to tell them that she would be coming along with the children to see them.

Queen Jenny complimented me by saying, "Fabulous! You are looking my boy; god should protect you from the girls in the future." She then started to get a glance at Ellena. She stated that Ellena was looking as awful as always. Ellena experienced a wave of emotions upon hearing this statement.

She was filled with disappointment, but I murmured into her ears, "Ellena I guess you are looking as good as always. Our mom is just joking." Probably she heard my words. Upon hearing my words, she got a shine in her eyes. I wondered what might have given her such a bright shine in her golden eyes.

She hugged us both and prayed for our long lives. She took us in front of the kings. Lord Elvin stared at me and was delighted to see me.

King Jon introduced me as the son of Mr. Stark and Mrs. Stark and Ellena as her daughter. He stated, "he is the only son of Mr. Stark and Mrs. Stark. he is 7 years old. According to him, he wishes to join the Warrior's school when he turns 10. And this is my only daughter, Ellena, she is currently 8, and she will also be joining the school 3 years from now." Lord Elvin told us both that he also had a daughter of our age. He added that it would be great if we 3 got together.

He held my hand and asked me to play with her daughter the next time they came. He added he had not brought her because she did not like to talk to other people. I told him that every person likes me and wants to have a chat with me. This gave him a burst of great laughter.

However, he knew that his laughing at me might end up hurting me, so he assured us that the next time he visited he would be bringing his daughter to Raisens.

14

THE OTHER KINGDOMS!!!!

***

(Year 991 A.G. Place-Jade)

Jade is one of the great nations in our world. Jade is ruled by King Moraine. He is the 7th lord of jade.

He called a summit between the nations, Glob and the Jade. Moraine's only purpose in life was to conquer the whole world and rule over it all by himself. He needed a huge army to take over the other great nations. Glob was the nation most suitable for the population increase in the army.

Glob was a nation, which was scattered all over the continent.

Glob isn't so beautiful place to live in. As the name itself suggests, the citizens are stinky goblins. They have created underground shelters all over the continent. It is a pain in the head when it comes to identifying their bases. Their population rate is high and the birth rate is even higher.

Goblins are of 2 types.

1.

Human eaters

These goblins like to eat humans, not because they are starving but because they just get fun out of it. They have pointy ears, green or brown skin, and long, crooked noses that characterize it. Goblins are known for their cunning nature. They have no emotions or sympathy for others.

They typically inhabit caves or other underground spaces. Despite their reputation for mischief, they generally spent their days and nights in underground caves.

1.

The Mora Goblins.

They are the same as the human eaters but they had offered their lives to Moraine. They want to live in the open air, where there is no one around. They have already collaborated with Moraine.

Some of them went to attend the summit at Jade. The one who was the most curious to collaborate was the goblin "Globin". Globin was the prince of all the goblins. He had great physiques, unlike other fatty goblins.

It is said that when he was a child of only 10.

He pierced the neck of the actual prince and declared himself the prince and future king. Nobody in the globs was able to put a question against that ruthless child.

He was feared by the goblins.

****

(About Jade and Moraine)

Jade was an exceedingly large kingdom. He matched Raisens in terms of area. Jade was ruled by Moraine. Moraine was a 55 years aged man. All the populace was referred to as humans; these people didn't have any special ability like us. They were just mere flesh-holding people. The only one who had the special ability was Moraine.

CHAPTER SIX

THE ABILITIES OF GREAT MANIPULATOR 'MORAINE'!

Moraine was known for his prowess in manipulation. When he was 29, he was announced the king of Jade by his father. His father's last words were one of the reasons why he started starving to rule over the world.

His father the 6th king said to him, "This world shall know you, Moraine. This world was made by the gods to be ruled by our family, the only thing you have inherited from me is my will, don't let this spark fade in you, let the spark come out from you and burn those who come to stop you.

RISE higher and higher above this heavenly body."

He then started to murmur to himself and after his chanting finished he started to laugh balefully. He then asked his son to lend him his ears, he kissed his ears and said "CURSE".

Just after he said, he died. It is said that his father cursed him; this curse lent him the power to manipulate.

****

(The Great Power of Curse)

The power is renowned as "Manipulatism". His power lets him manipulate the person, whom he touches. After he has touched your body, even if a bit, his Genjutsu will be imposed on you. Nobody has ever escaped his Genjutsu as of now. His grandfather used the same technique and the same curse, nevertheless the father of lord Elvin was able to defeat him in a 1vs1 duel with ease. Elves are actually fast and very skilled; he was able to take him down easily, without any struggle.

The only way was to fight him in long-range and use a long-range weapon to maintain a distance. This would eventually decrease the chances of you encountering him directly.

The only way he can catch you under his ultimate Genjutsu is physical contact between you and him. That is the only flaw in this curse.

CHAPTER SEVEN

THE TRAINING BEGINS

(*Raisens, year 994 A.W.*)

It was the start of the New Year. As planned, Ellena and I got into the warrior's school. In our first class, we were told that there would not be any regular classes instead, we would be told the timetable before the day of lessons. I still remember the teacher telling us, "There are high chances that the school will be working all day and night, if someone wants to learn more than enough, feel free to ask. Great warriors are not born but they are built."

She pridefully added, "Nobody is born a warrior, in the same way that nobody is born an average man." Her voice faded because I was not paying attention to her at all, instead, I was glaring at the king's daughter, Ellena.

I was 10 and she was 11 now, maybe I fell in love with her.

She was kind, beautiful, supportive, empathic............................

She treated me with all the care that I starved for. From my childhood, I always stayed with her at all times. She was one of the few people who didn't bully me.

***

I guess when we grin, laugh, and talk together, we start to have feelings for each other. We start to feel optimistic; we start to admire each other with all our hearts. Love is one of the best feelings created by God.

However, only unconditional love is the best one. It is a pure and selfless form of love that is transmitted freely without any strings attached. Unconditional love is characterized by acceptance, forgiveness, empathy, and willingness to support and care for the other person, regardless of their flaws or mistakes.

This love is the only powerful force that can bring people closer, together, and create deep and meaningful connections.

****

Soon, Ellena noticed my eyes and asked the purpose of my staring at her. I just nodded my head and smiled, she smiled too. She told me, "Tyler, I guess you should focus on what the mistress says rather than glaring at me, I guess that's the best we can do as of now." I totally agree with her, it is no use staring at her if I could not tell her how I feel, I know when I would ask her out- when things would settle down properly, I thought. This gave me a sigh of happiness.

CHAPTER EIGHT

THE GREAT LIBRARY

It was the same day when we, the students were asked to gather in the library area.

***

Our school has an impressive open area for sword and weapon practice. The school itself was massive, with multiple areas where one could perfect their skills and abilities.

The open area was large enough to accommodate multiple groups of students at once, with a wide variety of training equipment and weapons available for use.

The library contained thousands of tomes. Our teacher gave a brief introduction about her, continued, and continued telling us about herself. All of a sudden, she got into a strange motion; this got her the attention of all of us.

"I know most of you are 11 already, so I guess it's the best time for you all to unleash your abilities. 3 months from now you all will be given the 'Power Enhancing Juice'. Moreover, by tomorrow let me know which weapon you prefer to use. As of today, I will be teaching you about the past events, no need to lower your enthusiasm." After 2 hours of lecturing, I got to know nothing new. Ellena's mom had been telling us that all as bedtime stories. I felt drowsy a hundred times; if only Ellena was not there to scold me, every time I got myself drowsy, she would hit me on my head. My eyes really got dead.

The following night I asked Ellena which weapon she would prefer to use. In response, she said, "Hhmmmmmmmm!! Tyler, I am all muddled, I cannot choose a heavy weapon because It would drain my energy faster, I guess I would go by, sword and bow-arrow. I can learn special arrow styles, and also to use a sword." Well her statements filled me with bewilderment. I was clueless about what arrow types meant. Ellena asked me with a sigh, "Tell,

tell Tyler what you prefer more..." I interrupted her in between and asked to get herself some rest, I was able to catch a sight of her tiredness.

27

At last, I gave it a thought, "what the best weapon could be for me, well, swords are sharp, and have some exceptional advantages. Axes are keen too but I am not so powerful to hold a huge weapon. OH god!! it's damn so confusing." finally after wasting much of my precious night's time and came to an ultimate conclusion, "I will choose the same as Ellena chooses."

CHAPTER NINE

THE WEAPON SELECTION

The next morning Mistress Jenny woke me up. She was already with the breakfast for me; Ellena was able to get herself up, early in the morning, all by herself.

I was not even able to wake myself up and tell everyone that I would be the next future king, I pep-talked every kid about how to be the king, is so ironic isn't it? Just after, I gained consciousness, the first thing Mistress Jenny asked me about was, "Tyler, I am so curious to know what weapon you prefer."

I was speechless. Well, she must have not expected to get an overwhelming answer. Well the main reason for my speechlessness was, that I didn't have any specific suggestions on weapons, weapons are weapons, they are used to cut the throats of enemies, I questioned myself, "Was it really important to choose the weapons, why can't I learn each and every weapon?"

Mistress Jenny started to stare deep inside my eyes and answered me, "Becoming a skilled swordsman is no easy feat, - it requires years of dedication and hard work. Only through persistent practice and determination can one hope to master the art of the sword."

Well, I almost forgot that she could read the minds and hearts of people. Well after I remembered this I asked her for help.

I asked her to look into my heart. Well she raised both of her hands wide and then held my neck with her left hand and put her right hand on my chest. Well, it really felt good. She then looked into my eyes and busted into laughter. It was so embarrassing; I asked her the reason for the giggling. In response, she got serious and asked me in a slightly enraged voice, "How dare you! You started to like my daughter; I am really pissed off by your behavior now you shall know pain and suffering." She added, "Your days of suffering start from this very glance."

I was really in anguish, at her statements. I was about to ask her, for her pardon.

All of a sudden, she again started giggling. She then, with an emphatic voice told me, "I guess your love for Ellena is unconditional, but you know her, she isn't that type of girl, there are very few chances that she will have the same feelings for you as you have for her, but I know her care towards you far surpasses mine for you." I thought, "Hmmm! Does she really care about me?" "Obviously I do" she insisted holding my hands together. In response, I also told her that I care for her too.

Can the things get more embarrassing than this?

Ellena entered the room to get me. Queen Jenny was sitting just next to me on my bed; we were holding each other's hands tightly.

Ellena widened her eyes with astonishment.

At last before Ellena and I were about to leave, Mistress Jenny called us both and gave both of us a tight loving hug.

31

CHAPTER TEN

THE POWERS!!!!

Ellena did not ask me about what she saw; maybe she had unwavering faith in her mother.

***

The women of Raisens are most loyal and faithful followed by Elves. Elf-women are so loyal that they only marry once in a lifetime.

***

Ellena and I started to move towards the library. We were instructed to gather in the library. That day we were asked about our choices,

I made the same choice, special arrow styles, and swords. We were then provided with interesting information, once we mastered the weapons we could go to the "Fantasy Forest." During the break, I asked Ellena, "Hey Ellena, how if we go to see the fishes at the lake?" she rejected my proposal and asked me if I could join her to see the weaponry equipment instead. "This is a greater idea" I responded.

That day Ellena and I somehow managed to infiltrate into the weaponry section.

It really felt good doing kinds of stuff like that with her. We were surprised to see the weapons.

There were hundreds of swords and axes, hundreds of lances, and thousands of spears and arrows.

I was amazed to see the arrows, they all were the same, the same construction, I wondered, if they all were the same how the warriors use different types of arrow styles. I asked Ellena out about this, she said, "You are as dumb as always, the warriors who use the fire release or water release or raw strength as their abilities, these abilities take some time to recharge.

The arrow styles let you fill the normal bow with your powers, by doing so, a warrior's power does not replenish fast and he can use it by using a bow and arrows.

Many warriors use these styles, like my father, he fills the arrow with his raw strength; this not only increases the speed but also enhances the destructive power."

Well, I should have admitted that, 'if she were to become a teacher she would become a great one.'

Her explanations were as good as always. After our exploration, we got our senses back and noticed that it was evening already. Moreover, we missed our afternoon meals. By the time we reached the palace, it was already around 7.

CHAPTER ELEVEN

THE GREAT SORROW PART-1

It was a splendid day. Ellena and I both agreed to get ourselves to the nearby mountain. We both marched toward the mountain, talking out things that didn't have much meaning. We talked about 'how to fight in a war'........'when to go to The forest of fantasy'......'what is better? a griffin or Phoenix'...... 'best mythical creature' 'best abilities....'.........and blah... blah.... Blah.... Blah.

In the end, after the arguments, we finalized that both Griffins and Phoenix were the best mythical creatures.

After 3 hours of long climbing, we finally reached the place.

"Serenity descends upon a majestic mountain, tall and firm, adorning a mantle of deep emerald greens. Grand trees grace its surface, as whispers of ancient tales echo amidst the rustling leaves, cascading serenity into the cool breeze.

Blooms in myriad hues grace the land with a blush,

poppies red as love,

lilies as pure as morning dew, carpeting the land in a picturesque hue." I said to Ellena, Ellena busted into laughter. She admitted the beauty of the pond and the flowers that were there.

She said, "Tyler, this place really looks mesmerizing, I just love this place, once we get our equipment and weapons we can use the place to train ourselves, don't you think we should give this place a name?" well I just nodded to whatever she said. Though it had to be beautiful it took me 11 days to find that place. At last, we named it "The Place of Love".

We both drank the water from the crystal clear pond. The grass was as soft as cotton, I insisted. And asked Ellena if we both sleep together there. In response, she shouted to the top of her voice, "Okay Tyler". It was evening when we both woke up. My hairs were filled with the pieces of grass.

Although Ellena's hair was as good as always, mine were really in a bad condition.

As I stood in front of the pond, the sky above turned into a mesmerizing canvas of red hues as the sun set in the distance. The reflection of the sky on the calm waters of the pond created a breathtaking scene that left me in awe. It was as if I was witnessing a work of art being painted right before my eyes. All of a sudden Ellena came closer and closer to me as if she was about to kiss me. I closed my eyes but I was wrong she started to remove the grass pieces from my head. At that moment her face looked prettier than the sun itself.

Suddenly a thought came to mind, 'if I fear of not telling my feelings she won't get to know the feelings.'

After these all thoughts, I held Ellena's hands softly and told her, "Ellena you are the girl I love……".

CHAPTER TWELVE

THE GREAT SORROW PART-2

*"Tyler I see you more of a family than a lover",
Ellena said softly. She removed her hands from
mine. She then started to go down the hill all
by herself. Though I didn't know what to say or
what to do I followed her.*

*I kind of knew that I messed up, but didn't
know how much. I thought, "Maybe it would
take time for her to understand how I felt for
her, maybe things would get normal from
tomorrow onwards" and I thought and thought
until we reached home.*

*She and I both entered the room. We both were
quiet but I was quieter.*

Soon Ellena's mom arrived at our room, at first she was overjoyed but after she noticed our faces she immediately paused her rhythm, and said, "Well Tyler, tomorrow is the day isn't it?" and I nodded at her. Ellena got furious and asked the queen to ask me to leave.

I was appalled by what she said and left the room silently. Her mother got the gist of what I had done. Her mother asked Ellena, "What's the matter and why ask him to leave?" she told her about all things, 'the place of love' and about the proposal.

Well, I was just outside the room at the door with my ears straight. Her mom said, "Hmmmmm so that's something I thought would happen sooner or later but there is nothing we can do now........" In between Ellena taunted, "You want me to do nothing about this messed up stuff, Mom?". That's not what I wanted to say, I wanted to suggest you that at least you could talk out the stuff with him and sort out the mess. "Why should I, just tell me why should I, it's no age for doing these kinds of things, I want to be the next heir to the throne.......".

"You are already the princess and the rightful person to have the realm, Raisens……"

"What are we actually arguing for, instead of explaining things to Tyler you are after me, I don't think a mother should suggest things like this." To this queen, Jenny was left speechless, and after thinking for a while she asked, "By the way how you about Tyler?"

"I saw him as a part of my family not as some friend or buddy, he is kind, and understands others' sufferings. I didn't want him to ask me out like that, maybe if we had been grownups, then too I would have declined him right away. Well now nothing can be changed, once the trust is broken it can't be repaired." "Are you alright", "Absolutely fine" said Ellena.

"Okay then, good night, and all the very best for tomorrow." And the Ellena went to her bed. I heard all their talks with my ears and got the gist of what *was going on. I was really heartbroken, from listening to their talks. I moved aside from the door of our room as I heard the voice footsteps getting louder. Queen Jenny came out of my room and asked me to explain all the things to her. I explained to her each and everything.*

After listening to my words she got anger-filled and slapped me on the face. And said, "How dare you did that to my girl, you are nothing more than a scum."

Tears started falling from my eyes as she continued, "I didn't think you would do something like that to the daughter of a king and queen. And now I ask you to stay away from my precious daughter. Clear or not."

And I answered her in a shaking voice, "Ccc...leaarrr..." and then she left the place leaving me crying.

****

(Inside Ellena's room)

Ellena was present at the door, the other side where I was crying, she whispered to herself, "Mom, you shouldn't have got that far" and then she got back to her bed.

****

I always thought that after the death of my parents, the queen and king would treat me as their child and Ellena would always be with me, but that day I understood that my thoughts were wrong and so were my assumptions.

The only thought that came into my mind was to leave that place forever.

I murmured to myself, "Why did things end up like this.... Why ....why...... how......why?"

For me leaving the palace seemed to be the best option. At that time all I was thinking was, 'I believed, I had a special place in their hearts but I was mistaken, I was nothing more than an entertainer to them and now is the time for the show.'

I planned my plan,

firstly, I would leave the place and would go to the kingdom of elves, Elfins.

THE GREAT SORROW PART-3

I was in the hallway sobbing and weeping my tears. "what do I do?......... why can't I get the unconditional love that I have for them?" I asked. Suddenly one of the king's guards came and saluted and said, "Good morning Mr. Stark, how was your night?" This led me to burst into tears.

The king's guard sat beside me and said with a sweet tongue, "Mr. Stark now you are 11, if Your Majesty, if Ma'am Ellena saw you like this she would make fun of you."

*****

Well, he was doing nothing but taunting me, because I and Ellena always remained together.

*****

This didn't have much impact on me, I was still crying. The king's guard then asked me, "Mr. Stark will you be happy if I give your sword and equipment earlier than your majesty?" "well if I get my sword and other equipment now it would be easier for me to leave the kingdom, also it's still midnight and it would at least take 5 hours for the sun to show itself." I thought.

I nodded my head. The king's guard got his breath back. He stood up and took me to the royal storeroom. He told me that only the royals of the palace and apart from the royals only he was allowed to enter there. That place wasn't dirty like the other store rooms were. There was a royal table, where the weapons for me and Ellena were placed.

These weapons were to be taken by us later that day. Well, I saw 2 swords in their covers and 2 sword belts 2 bows, and 15 arrows of white and blue colour each. I asked him which was the sword I was supposed to use. He pointed towards one of the two swords. I took the other sword.

"Well that sword is meant for the use of Your Highness, and also it has her name written on it." Yeah, that was true, on the ricasso of the sword it was written, Ellena...... I ignored him. I took all the sword's material and told him that I was going to sleep now.

"Okay", he said and murmured "Strange kid".

The sword was really beautiful. The word had a very comfortable grip, the pommel was made up of gold and the grip was made up of high-quality fabric. The sword wasn't much heavy though had perfect sharpness. The quillon of the sword was also made up of gold and platinum. The cover and belt were made up of flexible and high-quality fabric.

The whole sword structure was the same to that of mine. I took Ellena's sword on purpose, 'to remember her, to remember her even during fights, so that even if I were to be alone I would remember who filled my broken heart'. My heart was already broken when I was younger than those 11 years, but she and her family broke it into even smaller pieces.

CHAPTER FOURTEEN

THE DEAD MEN'S PLACE PART-1

"It had been an hour since I have left the palace...... where do I go.... To the east, or the north." I was all confused. All I wanted was to get myself to a place where I could learn how to fight and how to be a true warrior.

All of a sudden I remembered that in the east there is a residence of all elves. Then I realized I was moving opposite to the east. On the first day only, I wasted 2 precious hours of mine.

On my way towards the east, I found an old house, made up of fine quality wood, had windows, 2 floors, huge wooden gate, the house was covered with plant growth.

But something was odd about the house, the winter hadn't come but a strange cold breeze was coming from the house. It felt like, 'I was in a necropolis'.

"As an upcoming, I must check this house; the house might contain ghosts or something like that but I must not lose my courage", I thought.

My legs moved on their own and stopped right in front of the house. I read a notice on the gigantic door of the house it said, 'Do to enter, highly dangerous...... might lose your life.'

But I entered the house and was dejected to find no one in the room. The inner house was well-managed and had antique items. The house was decorated and had all sorts of furniture. Suddenly my eyes got onto a bluish intangible leather-made rope that was hanging.

I tried to grab it but my hands moved through it. I raised my eyes to the top and Abruptly an intangible human jumped from the roof to the ground right in front of my eyes.

Looking at his distinct face and the color of his skin, I lost consciousness.

"What a miserable brat, he is"

"Oh darling what makes you say so......"

"He entered our place without permission and got pleasured by seeing the beauty of these beloved antique showpieces of mine"

"My grandson, do you really believe that if a child watches your beloved antiques unintentionally, you get the right to kill that kid, Ms. Meadow, my grandson's wife, shouldn't have used your spells on him"

"Well grandfather I didn't cast my spells on him"

"well great-great-grandfather, he just collapsed down on seeing grandpa, I guess he just ran away from his home, and he has his sword, maybe he's........."

"Hey you, my beloved grandson, come down from the roof and undo your gravitation ability"

"Anyways let's check him, in order to get some information about him"

Emma Meadow moved towards me in order to check my sword and other things I wore. She first inspected my legs, then the pants, then the shoes, then my hands, and then she moved to check my sword.

She took the sword from my scabbard and started examining it, she commented, "Nicely built, great sharpness, neither so heavy nor too light, comfortable grip, but wait there is something written on its ricasso."

"What is it, my dear Meadow"

"It's written, Ellena"

The boy replied, "Ellena you say isn't she the daughter of the current king and queen."

The oldest one asked, "Isn't she a Meadow too from her mother's side."

"Well, she is, but how come he has her sword?"

Then she moved towards me and checked the rest of my body, she also got a pendant from my neck.

Well not much after they saw my sword I was categorized as a thief.

But Emma Meadow defended me as she knew I was a Stark. And I actually was.

"A Stark, you say grandma; how do you know this?"

"Well he has a pendant with contains a ring in it and on the inner side of this golden ring, it is written 'I'm Stark'"

Great-great grandfather suspected me, "Maybe the ring also does not belong to him and he just stole it from the only left Stark boy."

"Well that's not true grandpa, the pendant is made up of the purest gold that only Meadows or the Starks have, also the ring was specially built by me for the dearest friend of yours, and also I can see magical enchantments on it done by me."

"Grandma is right; I can see them too"

"Well grandson, you should not defend your grandma, we all know that Meadow girls don't lie, and even if she were to lie, I would still have believed my beloved darling."

Then they both shared a warm and loving kiss.

Great-great Grandfather asked them not to do it in front of their grandchild. But they were so busy in themselves.

So in order to change the topic he asked, "What to do with this only left poor Stark kid?"

CHAPTER FIFTEEN

THE DEAD MEN'S PLACE PART-2

The youngest one replied, "What good can this boy get to us? We have been dead for ages now, I don't think he is of any use, we can finish him off, can't we?"

"Nobody will lay their fingers on him", told the great-great-grandfather furiously.

"Yes, we can't take someone's life like that, also he neither had committed a crime nor he is accused of something," said Emma Meadow in order to defend my life.

"Well, he must be very dear to the royal people of Raisens and the king himself." The husband to Emma Meadow laughingly commented, "If

he is the only Stark then he is richer than the king alone, he must be having more than enough money to live luxuriously."

The great-great-grandfather laughingly said, "Hahahahahhahahahhh... Well, he surely is stark, he wears a plain shirt of silk and no armor, if it is to talk about this kid's richness, he can buy more than half of the Raisens by only selling his collection of jewels that he has in the Magica, the safest bank to ever built in history."

Emma Meadow commented, "This kid is a true menace, if he lands into wrong hands or gets deteriorated, he can cause harm to only to our beloved empire also to other kingdoms, so we must counsel him."

"count me out then, I am bad at giving advice." said the youngest one.

"That's why ended up young", taunted his grandfather.

And everybody busted into laughter. Their voices disturbed my nap. I got back my consciousness. As I got it, I lifted my spine from the floor.

And what I saw was unimaginable, I was witnessing the live but dead man; a ghost. Every one of them didn't had legs and were floating around 7 inches up the floor and their complexion wasn't fair rather bluish. Their bodies were translucent, I couldn't my eyes.

There was one woman who got my attention, she had very long hair, in order to check if I was in my dreams or not I stood up and lifted my hands towards her breast in order to touch her bluish hair.

But my hands slipped through her athletic chest. Precipitously her intangible body transformed into human flesh. She in a flash grabbed my hand and told me with sarcastic politeness, "ohhhh, you cute boy, don't just use your hands like that, the men from an honourable house shouldn't be doing these kinds of criminal acts."

She patted my back with her hands, I was in shock and asked them, "well are you the angels that come to take people when they die, and also please do let me know if I am dead, if am dead so also tell me how I died...............?"

"Well It doesn't matter how I died, now I won't be able to go to the forest of fantasy" I added.

"Forest of .... you say, according to the rules you cannot go there alone, you should be going there with a partner" the youngest one told me.

"I know, but I wish to go there by myself." I added, "By the way you didn't tell me who you are, did you??"

CHAPTER SIXTEEN

THE DEAD MEN'S NOVELLA PART-1

The eldest of them of all told me, "Your choice kid, but the way that leads there isn't safe, and I heard that the goblins have got more active than they were before, they have started to come out of their dark caves." He added, "Though you look more than enough skilled to survive their attacks, you still are weak, you are a Stark, they get better as they age, only if you were a year older, you would have shown them their right places."

Well, I got myself in confusion, how would it benefit me only if I'm a year older?

So I asked him, "What magic would happen the next year?"

"You really know very less about the Starks, a Stark unleashes his abilities only after 12 years of age, his abilities are strong and sometimes unique, it happened many a time that the ability unleashed by a Stark is completely new, also you share more life energy than the Raisens, around half of a healthy Elf."

'Though my parents died so young.' I thought.

Suddenly the beautiful lady replied, "Your parents lived many good years, we watched them grow from this very dead house, they used to visit us often and would talk about you, your growth, your likes and dislikes as a child......"

'All they did was talk about me' I thought. These thoughts lead me to burst into tears. The youngest one said, "Poor boy warriors don't cry."

The third male said, "Warriors and men do cry."

"Well, it's time for introductions." The eldest told us.

The eldest one started first and we got ourselves silent.

He began, "I am Clarke, Russo Clarke, I belong from the house Clarke, I died because of my injuries, a long time back, around 250 years ago now. I was the one who brought peace to the people, to the people of Raisens. I fought in the battle against Moraine of the Jade. I defeated his 10000 men all by myself.

I was the dearest friend to your great-great-grandfather Robert Stark.

I used magic spells as my special ability. I could do elemental spells, which let me use the power of all 5 elements along with lightning, light, and darkness. When I was 13, I bonded with a Phoenix. I married Bylana Stark of the house Stark, at the age of 21. I belonged to the house of Clarke and was their leader for about 49 years. I died at the age of 95."

***

(Description of Sir Russo Clarke)

Even as a ghost he looked not so old, had only a few wrinkles on his face. He stood tall, about 6 feet and 3 inches, had muscular hands, and a muscular body, though it seemed they had weakened a little. His hairs were white, from his birth. All people of the house Clarke are white-headed. He was a renowned warrior; his instincts were nowhere to be found at that time. His face was elegant, had straight hair, and purple eyes. He used a sword, magic wand, and long magical stick- 'Worddo' as his weapons.

***

The next one to introduce was his grandchild.

He began, "I am Draken Clarke from the house Clarke. I unleashed my abilities at the age of 10 only. I was able to pull or push the objects, I can also control the speed of it. I was the only hand of the to ever exist only after Lord Robert Stark."

***

(Description of Draken Clarke)

He looked exceptionally good and had an elegant facial structure. He was 6 feet tall and did not so a muscular body but his muscles had great muscle density. The hairs he had were as white as the snow and his eyes were as blue as the sky.

***

Up next was my favorite one among all of them, lady Emma Meadow from the house of the Meadows, she was the late wife of Draken Clarke. She began with her honey voice, "I am Emma Meadow from the house Meadow, I have not given any special name for my special ability, but I can see through someone's mind and heart, use magic for doing enchantments, magic for healing, and finally I also use magic of Light. All Meadow girls have the ability to see through the thoughts of people."

I remembered something from the name of her house and I started to murmur to myself, "Ohhhhh.... A Meadow......... I know of their house ..., how......... oh yes! She is from the same house as Queen Jenny."

I was in shock and I got even more shocked after I asked her how she was related to Jenny, "well you see kid, the girl you are asking about is my first granddaughter, she also serves as the queen of the Raisens."

***

(Description of Mistress Emma Meadow)

She was a young woman of 39, with a radiant personality that shone through her golden hair and golden eyes. Standing at 5 feet 7 inches tall, she had a commanding presence that drew people towards her. Her hair flowed down to her waist in shimmering waves, and her eyes sparkled with warmth and kindness. Despite her age, her youthful energy was contagious. Her voice was soft and soothing. Her confidence and strength were evident in the way she carried herself, and her grace and elegance were undeniable. She had the same eyes as Queen Jenny. She was a woman of substance, with a heart full of love and compassion. She was truly a rare gem that anyone would be lucky to know.

***

At last, it was the turn of someone who seemed to be a disturbing element and also the youngest fellow. The boy looked no more than a warrior who was in his twenties.

He first got himself on the table and then he began to tell me, about himself, "Long time back, it was a stormy night, guess what......... that day I was born. When I came into this cursed world even the lightning in the sky roared, and the trees fled away by the high winds. All of this settled down with my first cry. I am Robin Clarke of House Clarke, I have the ability to change the gravitational force between the objects, any humans, or any other entity. If I just focus a little on any object and use my ability that object pulls all the objects near to it. I used the same ability to stand on the roof when you entered our house. I was a lovable character, though I died young."

He was the only one who had the most aura inside of him to tell me about himself. His efforts in teaching me about his super cool special ability made him my favorite one among all of them.

CHAPTER SEVENTEEN

THE DEAD MEN'S NOVELLA PART-2

Summing up all of this mess, here are all of the things you need to know about them.

The eldest one is Russo Clarke. Uses magic and .... her wife is Bylana Clarke.

The grandchild of Russo Clarke is Draken Clarke. His wife is Emma Meadow. He also uses magic and...........

Emma Meadow is the great-great-grandmother of Jenny Meadow (Queen of Raisens).

Her grandchild is Robin Clarke. Robin Clarke had his lover, Emily Katz, who was the great-

great-grandmother of King Jon Katz (King of the Raisens). Robin Clarke didn't like her much and got married to someone else.

Emma Meadow gave back my sword and asked me why hadn't I enchanted it yet. I replied, "Well you see I am leaving this place, for my own good, also I didn't have time to get it enchanted." "In that case, I would be delighted to help you kid," told Mistress Emma Clarke.

"Well my grandmother is the best enchanting caster of her time, nobody even today comes closer to her skills." Mistress Emma Clarke went upstairs after taking my sword back from me. I was then asked several questions about my tragic past. At last, I asked Sir Russo Clarke, if he felt alone because he didn't have her love of life with him, to which he refused and told me, "Stop thinking that I am alone and lonely like you, my dear Bylana is sleeping upstairs."

I asked Robin Clarke the same, in response he chose silence over revealing. Sir Draken Clarke murmured into my ears, "Don't ask him questions related to his love life."

CHAPTER EIGHTEEN

THE GUARDIANS OF RAISENS!!

After an hour of chit-chats, Emma Meadow returned to us with my sword and a brand-new scabbard. She was practically glowing with happiness and her excitement was contagious. She looked very satisfied, I was able to feel the aura that came from the leather scabbard. The leather of the scabbard contained a shiny green jade. The jade was embedded beautifully in it. Mistress Emma Meadow blushed at me as I saw the delicate curve of her fingers that gave me the impression of slender elegance (Though I was looking at my sword.). she came to me and handed over the scabbard into my hands. Then she started telling me about the magic, she used to enhance my majestic sword.

She started with joy, "The magic I used is the most purified type of magic to ever exist, the magic of light. I used it to add some feeling into the sword, this would drastically increase the bonding with your sword. Your sword will come flying to you, no matter how far you are from your sword. Also I used the lighting magic to increase its sharpness, and I also used the magic from the light to increase its endurance. Your sword won't get blunt no matter how you use it. Now your main task with your sword it that you have to learn how to use it properly, and use your time efficiently from now on. And also I forgot to mention you can now attach the scabbard rope to pull your sword back." I had many doubts about, 'how to call it when it's far away......... bonding what bonding.........' but I still nodded to whatever she told me.

In between Sir Robin Clarke took the scabbard from me and pulled the sword out of its scabbard.

Draken Clarke announced that the sword won't be given to me as usage of magic of light was banned for the enchantment of weapons. This made me a little raged, I thought, 'like I would listen to this half-dead person, oh wait!! This full dead person'. Just after I thought this, Emma Meadow chortled and then she put both of her palms on her mouth and said, "sorry" gently in a low voice. Her acts were very cute and matched to that of my Ellena.

Sir Russo Clarke said to Sir Draken Clarke, "it won't be an issue to send him with the sword, the magic can't be undone by any warrior apart from your dear wife, also all upper warriors would understand that my child, my Granddaughter-in-law, does the magic. Plus, this boy is a Stark, no one questions a Stark." I was glad that the eldest one spoke for me. It was clear to me that the Starks had something that made us unique from all other people of the Raisens. I asked him about this. In response he solidified his blue hand and put that on my shoulder and continued, "House Stark had always been the most honoured house. It had been more than 980 years since the Starks got their special status. A Stark won't kneel or even bow his head down in front of the lords or kings. Your House was massively rich, richer than any of our clans or houses, you are now the only one left of your pedigree, you are richer than the kings of our world, may be the richest kid to ever exist. You can live your life; any way you like or love."

But I wasn't told that I was that rich. I said to them with surprise, "but I was told that I didn't have any kind of money, that my parents left, the king told me that, my parents had a huge loss because of the drowning of our ship, which had all of our jewels." "a single ship is not enough to fill all of your jewels and also, all of your family's gold and jewelry had always been in Magica," said Robin Clarke.

"That means the king had broken his oath, an oath that the kings of Raisens have been taking, to not to lie, plus the person is lied to is a Stark and also he had disrespected house Stark and had also disrespected our very first king." Said Emma with a scowl on her face.

"Anyways, the king would have to answer about all of this" said Draken Clarke to Emma.

The eldest one, Russo Clarke asked me why I wanted to leave the Raisens. I told them everything, 'how the queen wanted me to leave........... about myself.........'

In between Robin moved upstairs and brought a silvery compass. After I finished, he gave me the compass and said with a sigh, "well this is my very first gift from my grandfather and grandma, I am handing over it to you, this compass won't get malfunctioned no matter what happens, return it to me when you return from your voyage. You should first have to go to the Magica and clear the things about your....... it is in the same direction; mid-way to the Elfins you would get the Magica."

I felt bad for him. I got permission to take the compass with me from his grandparents. In response sir Draken Clarke nodded his head in affirmation, and the mistress told to feel free to take it. At last, they all patted my back with their hands. I hugged Sir Robin and then I stepped forward to hug Lady Emma Meadow. Lady Emma solidified her whole body and hugged me the same way, how my Ellena did. In her ears, I whispered 'Thank you!'

CHAPTER NINETEEN

A NEW JOURNEY BEGINS!!

It was already 3 of the morning, I stepped out of their home and headed north.

I am Tyler Stark of the house Stark, and my real voyage begins now on.

I wore leather sandals that covered my legs to my ankles, silk-made long pajamas of dark blue color, and a green silk-made shirt, a royal one. And finally, I wore my pride and honor as I marched to the north. It was a moment I'll never forget. My first destination was the 'safest bank of the world- the Magica'. I read in the books that Magica is run by the dwarves of Alnor. They are known for their outstanding knowledge and skills in the art of forging. Some of the most famous weapons and pieces of jewelry were created by the dwarves. I would go to the Magica, claim what is mine, and seal my gold and diamonds for future use.

Faraway in the northwest, the goblins were called for the great summit again, king Moraine of Jade wanted to conquer the world, and for this to happen he needed men, powerful men but it was a fact that normal flesh was inferior to ours so they wanted to outnumber us by reproducing in their kind. He even joined shoulders with Goblin of the Glob. And everybody knows that the Glob is scattered all over the world.

Globin was their supreme leader who also wanted to rule, though he only wanted to rule his goblins.

***

(At the Jade Palace Year-995 A.G.)

"Lord Moraine of the Jade, you look well and good." said globin. Moraine cackled and said, "I just happen to not look in pieces, just like you,

hahaha............"

Suddenly they both got serious and Moraine asked him if they were ready to march toward the east. In response, the globin said with honor, "I have gathered 500 goblins with us and they will march towards the border of Raisens near the Magica."

"I would also send my 40 assassinators with you, I don't want any problems, kill the men, rape the women and girls, and also kill the guards and babies, this would tell them about our existence, this would develop fear in their hearts and they would immigrate to Raisens or Elfins, this would make us easy to attack them in near future, they won't be able to tell the kings and lords, that 150,000 men force is marching for their necks," said Moraine

***

The humans, people of the Jade were planning to attack us with all their forces, in the near future. Moraine the manipulator sent his 40 assassinators to ensure that the words of those 500 approaching don't spread before they burn down the small villages. These villages were built on the border between the Elfins and

Raisens to symbolize the friendship and brotherhood between the Elfins and Raisens.

I was now in the forest woods; it was already the orange early morning sky. I almost walked 11 miles in 2 and a half hours. Everybody in the castle must have woken up from their nightmares, everyone including my Ellena. I thought that they would come and find me, take me home. At least I expected this from Ellena but the question was 'when......??'

CHAPTER TWENTY

THE DAY I WAS BORN!!!

It was winter when I left the Raisens, the peak winters of Raisens, although the winters at Raisens were not that cold as one marches near to the Elfins, the weather gets worse and worse. The day I left the premises was the day, when the young warriors were to be provided with the 'Power Enhancing Juice' Also it was my birthday, on that day. I was full of myself, and marched north with all of my might, I expected Ellena to come and search for me.

****

(After 3 days of ....)

It was a cold chilling morning; I was expecting to get myself a lavish breakfast. According to my calculations, I must have marched for about 50 hours, about 200 miles. After my first day's march, I ate in the village of Raisens. I was half-empty for about 2 days. All I was expecting was a next village, where I could get a breakfast.

I practiced not to lose my directions without the compass, but every time I failed to keep my path straight. A skilled warrior shouldn't lose his directions, not always one have his compass. Whenever I lost my directions, I always thanked sir Robin Clarke for giving his beloved gift to me.

It was 3 days already but I couldn't hear the sound of the horses approaching. "May be they forgot, that I used to live in their daughter's room." I thought.

****

(In the Raisens Palace, the king with his queen were present in the room of Ellena)

"Well done my child, not only did you inherited all the special abilities of the honourable house of your mother, the Meadow but also unleashed your own ability" king Jon congratulated Ellena. She thanked him. Her mother continued, "you are now the light of the house Katz, and of meadows as well. You are just above outstanding, your highly calculative instincts, special combination of skill and will, power and finesse and an unmatched mental toughness. Ellena, you are exceptionally better than some of the warriors we know.

"You can read through the minds of people, you can use the raw magic of light, and also by time, you get to know more about the ability of your opponent. I heard many words of appreciation from your teacher, Jessica, she told me that you have the most potential of being a true warrior, a warrior who would eventually surpass our ancestors." Said Queen Jenny with a smiling face.

"By the way where is that Stark boy" asked the king to the queen.

"my dear the boy has been missing for past 3 days, I have sent your younger brother to search for him near the academy and near the palace as well."

"Well, you sent the royal king's guard to search for him!! I am calling him, send some ordinary warriors for him, I guess he must not have even unleashed his abilities." Said the king in a taunting way.

"yes my dear" responded the queen.

"I ask your leave, my beloved parents, I am not interested in your selfish talks anymore," said Ellena.

The royal kings guard that gave me the sword was the younger brother of the king. His ability is skin-changing. His ability isn't offensive but is best for infiltration, spying, and..........though he is also one of the best swordsmen in the Raisens.

CHAPTER TWENTY-ONE

THE DAY I WAS BORN!!!

Ellena was heading for the warrior's academy. On her way, the royal king's guard stopped her and asked her about me. She told him not to ask her about me, and added, "Also I am clueless about where Tyler has gone."

"The royals of Raisens are such a pain in the head." Said the younger brother of King Jon.

Saying this she continued to move on the path, the oath which was leading her towards the warrior's academy.

"Where would have Tyler ended up going to....... well it's not my matter of thinking. But he was like my family member........" she

thought as she walked. "Anyways, there is nothing I can do about it, the best thing for me to do is to focus on the classes. I need to get more powerful so that I can help the people of Raisens."

***

(In the warrior's academy, all students were gathered in the open field which contained standing wooden pieces that were too thick to cut, for sword training)

"So class today we are going to practice with our swords and axes. Those who are sword fighters go with Miss Jessica, and those who are in axes, come with me."

"So how are you all doing, I hope you all enjoyed yesterday's leave. Today we are going to the top of the mountain. We have a test for you all.........." Just after listening to this all students got dejected and replied to her words with large 'hiss' sound.

"students maintain the decorum!" she shouted at top of her voice and then politely continued, "Take it as a picnic rather than a test. So the

test is actually not a test but a test to test
your stamina, how you control your abilities,
your muscle strength and etc. etc........" she in a
politer voice "so all young students will march
towards the top of the tower with full energy, at
their top speed. And the one who will win will
get to go to the 'Forest of Fantasy' first. Not
to mention the first one will go there the next
year, not tomorrow."

"All you have to do is to run as fast as you
can, and reach the very top. Now to make it
difficult, all of you draw your swords out of
your scabbard, and now you all will run, having
your scabbard in one hand and the sword in
the other. "she further asked if anyone had any
doubts.

"Teacher, day before yesterday you told us
about that balance of muscles is necessary for
evolution of a warrior, some of us have heavier
swords than our scabbard, this test would
eventually strengthen our hands but unequally.
So in my opinion.........."

"Well, Technically, you are absolutely correct
about it, that's why we are going to do the same
tests daily. We would interchange the weights."

She further added, "I am glad that there is someone who listens to my lectures."

"Now enough of the discussion, the next time I say run, you all run." suddenly all of the students started running. "Good presence of mind" she murmured to herself.

****

"The inn looks better than the previous one. So finally it's time for breakfast." I was delighted after I finally reached the inn, in the deep forest woods.

"So what would you like to take, for breakfast," asked a girl. "well give me some vegetable soup, it should be as hot as the sun and should contain all necessary vegetables."

"Anything more......." she asked.

"I will let you know after I have my soup," I replied.

She told me to find myself a seat and asked me to wait for at least 10 minutes.

I sat on the last seat, near the window.

****

"So good morning my dear daughter, do you know, what I have got for your breakfast today?" The elf king asked his daughter.

"What? My beloved father."

"Well it's something that I like the most, in breakfast" commented the king.

"Not the vegetable soup, please no. I don't need it."

"Well as far as I remember, I used to like it when I was little......"

"And I hated it as ever" the Elf Queen said as she entered her daughter's room.

"yeah, that very well explain me why she hates it too."

"So what is our king doing here, babysitting" she taunted the king, Elvin.

"well my beloved love, I am his father sometimes I can get the breakfast for my daughter." Just after completing his words, he stepped forward towards the queen. Then they both kissed each other, kissing on the lips.

The room was all white as snow, the floor was made up of white marble, and the curtains were made up of linen, faux silk, and velvet of purple, blue, and red color. The room contained a large mirror on one side. The room was very big, the bed was made up of platinum and gold. It had an open balcony, from the balcony one could directly see the beauty of the large magnificent trees of Elfins. The trees, in different seasons, have different colours of leaves.

****

"Finally your wait is over...................."

"Tyler," I said.

"Finally your wait is over, Tyler," she said

I took the soup from her plate and started to check for spices that I liked. And 'yeah' I said with full satisfaction. "After starving for one and half days, the soup feels best." I thought as I drank it. The soup was really hot; it took me a total of 8 minutes to finish it.

I started making plans for my training, first I would have to increase my muscle strength and also have to work on stamina. Stamina is equally important as strength, if a warrior has a powerful ability but lacks stamina he might end up losing. Raw strength doesn't matter if you can't punch more than 200 punches in one go. The time period or the usage of the ability depends on stamina.

Nonetheless there are abilities that do not have a time period, they are everlasting, like magic of light or darkness, but still they consume your stamina. If the 2 fighters are fighting like cats and dogs, the one who is at his breath would lose.

"I am going to stay here for one day and night. Also if I don't give myself a proper nap today I might end up falling unconscious."

****

All the young students reached the top of the hill. Ellena was of course the first one to reach at the top. About Half of the students were at their breath and were panting and breathing heavily.

"well done, all of you, as promised the first ranker would be the first one to go to the Forest of Fantasy." Announced Jessica. She further told everyone that they would be learning to control their abilities in thinner air.

****

(The Goblins which were present in the summit, on the way back to their caves.)

"My king, should I send 500 of our men into their territory......."

"Absolutely no! You shit eater. We won't be sending our people for at least 1 month from today."

"But my king...." said one of the Goblin.

"Disobeying me means death! Don't you know this? I won't do whatever he wishes me to do, I am not his pet, we have got a bigger army than his."

"yes my lord, I totally agree with you," said another goblin. He further asked, the time when they would attack the people of Raisens and of Elfins.

"At least, after a month, as soon as we reach our home, prepare for the green magic."

****

"Anything else, Sir Tyler."

"No," I said.

"Well, you are young like me, and it seems to me that you are warrior, you are from which honourable house?"

"The most honorable one."

"you are a Meadow. That's nice."

"No, no you are mistaken about it, I am from the house Stark."

"Never heard of it before." She replied.

"You are from which house, mam?"

"I am from the house of Estrin. We have the most inns and places for tourists in Raisens. And around 2 in Elfins. I am the only daughter of the owner of all these."

"Nice, then why do you work here?" I asked her.

"Because I like to help others, that's why I help people like you."

"Help me, how?"

"do you have silver coins for the meal you just had?"

I checked, but I was pennyless. She saw me checking.

"say no more sir, from the House Stark. Your meals are on me, you stay here for as long as you want." She told me.

"why.........??" I asked her.

"You look above average to me, plus you are better than other drunkard people, who stay here, though they us, but still they are pain in my head."

"well then, I ask your leave."

"*Where to.......*"

"*For training.*" *I interfered with her in between.*

****

"*Well, it's time for your lessons my daughter.*" *Said the Elfins queen, Evelyn.*

"*Yes, Mom*" *she further asked what are the lessons she would be learning that day.*

"*Well my daughter, you have created friendship bonds with your Phoenix, so I would be checking both of your coordination as you fight my......*" *said the Elfins queen, Evelyn.*

"*say no more, let's hit the battlefield, dear Mom.*"

"*Get ready then, you have 10 minutes......*" *told the Elfins queen, Evelyn.*

"*Got it.*"

After getting ready, they both headed for the nearest mountain.

******

The Phoenix is really very powerful, if compared to, most of the creatures' in the Forest of Fantasy.

The Phoenix is an immortal bird that cyclically regenerates or is otherwise born again. A Phoenix obtains new life by rising from the ashes of its predecessor, he regains all of his memory. Though the Phoenix, she had was a newborn, a completely newborn, it was his first life.

A Phoenix is a majestic bird with brilliant red feathers that shimmer in the sunlight. Its wingspan is said to be enormous, and it is believed that the Phoenix can fly for long distances without getting tired. Whenever the Phoenix flies he leaves some burning particles behind, those particles can actually purify the air and can also provide the trees with the nutrition that they need. The Phoenix also merges with the body of its owner, temporarily, giving them the chance to have wings. The

Phoenix uses fire as their source of attack.

"So you are going to merge with your friend and reach the top. I will be watching over you with my Unicorn" told the Elfins queen, Evelyn.

"Merging, you say, I practiced that yesterday, 'Tails' are u ready to merge." Just after she said that, suddenly a very large phoenix came flying from the direction of the palace. Tails then shrank his size and sat on the shoulder of the princess.

"Hmmmmmm! But I wanted to sleep more, last night we both talked for too late......."

"I am sorry but we need to show our mom, how tough and strong we have got." Said the princess.

"Alright then, I guess it can't be helped."

I forgot to mention that the Phoenix can talk to people by using telepathic powers. There are other magical creatures also, which use it.

****

'The sky looks like an ocean of blood to me, when it sets off.' It was evening time and I was all in sweat. Just after I reached the inn, the same girl told me to get a bath. She herself showed me the directions to the hot spring of the inn. As I washed off my body, I thought, 'Oh yeah! it is going be my best night, tonight.' it was true when a person hadn't slept for 3 days and if he gets a warm bed, so he would definitely sleep like a log. After I was all set, I wore the clothes which were offered to me by the girl.

The girl looked about 2 years older than me. After I had my dinner, the girl straightaway took me to my room. The room was clean, well furnished, not royal but was good for an average person. She than told me not to waste time and also asked me not to dirty the blankets. Well, can help me put my......... "stop thinking dirty! I am not that type of girl, you pervert." She said in a raged voice. Just after saying that she left and she slammed the door close. "Maybe I was saying things in a wrong way, but now how I am going to sleep, I sat on the bed, my eyes staring the candle, at the table. Every night, I used to lay down on my bed, without my blanket on, Ellena always used to put blanket on me after I slept. "Did I lose *her?" I thought.*

After about an hour, I thought it would be meaningless, to think about it. So I placed my head on the cotton pillow, put the purple blanket on the body, and waited for the sleep to hit me. Not much later I was in deep sleep.

'I was in a place which had small flowers and beautiful plants, there were no traces of clouds, all clear sky. The sky seemed dark but yet everything was visible on the land, I was at. In my dream I looked up at the sky and was awestruck by the sight before me. I couldn't help but feel a sense of peace wash over me as I gazed up at the vast expanse of the universe above. I was alone at first, but then my eyes got onto a girl with long hairs, she was wearing a long royal dress just like a princess, she was none other than my Ellena. I ran towards her, and when I got closer, I raised my hand so as to touch her, to confirm that I wasn't sleeping. As soon as she held my hand, my dream automatically got destroyed.

I checked my hand, it was warmer than my left hand. It was still dark; the sun was about to rise. I slept again; in order to see her again.

I was going to leave that inn, that very morning but couldn't, after that night. I got hope, a sign that 'Ellena will come to get me'. I waited for a week, but not even a mere warrior came to find me. I practiced daily, hoped daily. Every night before sleeping, I thought and hoped for her to come. After so many hopes, I understood that I meant nothing to them and started my voyage to the Magica again.

****

(At the Raisens Palace)

"Any clues of that, bastard," asked King Jon in a detached and melancholic tone.

"No, my love, it seems that the boy has fled." replied the queen Jenny.

"He was dear to my friend, I must find him, I don't have to do anything with that boy, but because of my, late friend."

"Ask my little brother to find him, the king's guard should go himself to get him, and also tell my brother to teach him a lesson when he

finds him or else I would." Said the king, with every word his voice filled with rage.

"No need to tell me, queen, I heard him, from the deepest corner of the castle......"

"Was I that loud?" asked the king.

"No, my king but because I am your brother, I must keep one eye and ear towards you."

"Enough of talking already, my dear brother, go find that bastard before I wake up." told the king.

"Very well, I would leave at once, but I would wish to know what will you do to that boy." asked the king's younger brother.

"Nothing much, we would cease his property and jewels, and then beat him until he confesses his crimes, and if my mood gets bad after listening to his apologies I might end up sending him to one of the cells of my prison." Said the king.

"Do you believe that, after knowing this much I would take my man to get him?" Asked the king's brother.

"Of course you will, and of course I would do just as I told you." He further asked him to get back to his work immediately.

"I will, my lord. See you later, big brother."

There was someone else present there to listen to their talks. The person was none other than Ellena, she was present at the door.

The brother of the king had 70 personal warriors, who only took orders from the king or his younger brother. They all were renowned warriors. He ordered 40 of them to search for me, in the capital. And he himself marched with 10 of his man to find me outside the capital of Raisens.

CHAPTER TWENTY-TWO

THE POWER!!!

"You have become better than before, my dear Olivia, and your phoenix is outstanding." Said the queen of Elfins.

"she is not an object mom, she is my dearest friend, the only true one I have," Olivia said.

The phoenix then sat on the top of her head and hugged her head with her wings.

"Sorry, but I love both of you. For me, you both are my loving daughters and my unicorn is just like mother."

"Well, good to hear this from the queen of Elfins." Said the Unicorn. "Now let's back to our castle for lunch," said the mother of Olivia.

***

The Unicorn is known for its pure white coat, which shimmers and glows in the sunlight. Its horn is long and pointed, and it sparkles with a magical energy that can be seen from afar. The eyes of the magical white unicorn are large and expressive, with a deep, soulful gaze that seems to see into the hearts of those it encounters. The mane and tail of the magical white unicorn are long and flowing, often catching the breeze and fluttering in the wind. In terms of its personality, the magical white unicorn is known for its gentle and kind nature. It is a creature of great wisdom and compassion.

The magical white unicorn is also known to be incredibly fast and agile, able to run at great speeds and leap over obstacles with ease. Its grace and beauty are unmatched, and its movements seem to be imbued with a magical quality that is both mesmerizing and captivating.

***

It was nighttime, I climbed to the top of a sleeping tree. A sleeping tree is a special type of tree which have large leaves. Some trees of this species, by nature, create a large surface of leaves where large eagles or people can rest. The surface is soft, supported by the branches of the tree. I wasn't empty stomach, although I left the inn 10 days ago. I ate all kinds of nutritious fruits as I marched to..................... It was midnight, with a full moon sky, and millions of stars. I was at the top of the tree, and due to tiredness, I fell asleep really quickly. I was having the same dream that I had on the day when I was at the inn. 'she held my right hand with both of her hands, and tears fell from my eyes as I saw her beautiful luminous eyes, as she held my hands she said, "Why, Tyler".' Just after I saw her eyes in my dreams, my whole body lighted up, my body shinned like a white star, and the moment she said .... there happened a small explosion that released white shockwaves into the woods and the sky. When got my senses back, I was falling from the top. Though I didn't get much damage because of the soft surfaces created by the leaves, after felling I just lay on the ground, breathing heavily and panting. All I could think about was, the dream I had, and how I ended up falling from the top.

Thinking about it, my eyes filled with tears.

The next morning when I stood up and started to march again. Even after thinking too much, I didn't find the reason why I ended up falling from the top.

****

"Collect 500 of your man and march for Magica." Said the goblin's lord.

"But, lord you ordered us to move, after a month." Said one of the goblins.

"And now I order you to move immediately, got any problem, with it." Said their lord, violently.

CHAPTER TWENTY-THREE

THE DARKNESS ARISES

The days passed as I thought about her. I started to feel that heaviness inside me, there was something in my stomach that caused some feelings, feelings that I couldn't explain. That feeling made me powerless, the internal energy that kept us moving forward ended.

But still, I moved forward with a hope, a hope that I would live with Ellena. And yes the only thing that I wanted then, was to stay with her. All I wanted was to be happy, happy with her. 'I still wanted to do many things with her, we surely haven't done anything funny yet' I thought. I prayed to the gods, day and night, but it felt that either my words were low or I was just ignored by the gods. At last one person can't do anything but cry over it. The same thing I did.

As days passed, since I left the castle, I understood that a person is always alone if he just stops coming in front of the people he loves. That happens with everyone I guess, but yes there are always exceptions, but in my world, I was that exception; an exception that wasn't loved by the living people. All we wish is for at least one person who is scared to lose us. 'I had not gotten one' was the thing I thought. My heart started feeling heavier and heavier.

One night all of my sorrow busted into tears. I cried the whole night and at last, I stopped because my eyes got dry.

After losing my tears, I said one thing to myself, "Ellena knew, she always knew that I liked her, she just kept her eyes shut, she knew

I loved her but yet she said those mean words. Now it's time to show them the rage, the rage that shall burn their castle and royalness." And I shouted at the top of my voice, in rage. The rage inside me created the same shockwaves but this time in higher magnitude, this time the shockwaves removed the nearby trees completely, and a circular crater was formed, with me at the center.

Something was odd from then, I was able to move faster than before, able to swing my sword faster and with much more power. My stamina also increased drastically. At first, I thought it to be the outcome of my intense training, but it wasn't the case.

After 2 days of that event, I got highly motivated by the thoughts in my mind. I began to run, my speed kept on increasing and increasing. When I looked at my legs they were shining like a white star, I was able to feel that something was penetrating my legs. And when I stopped to check my legs, that glow was gone.

As days passed, whenever I used my muscles, they would start glowing white. And as days passed I understood that it was a special ability that let me do it.

After a week, I was able to finally understand what my ability was, my ability allows me to absorb nature's energy, not only to my muscles but also to my bones and every part of my body. I have read many books about our predecessors, no one has ever unleashed an ability like mine.

According to me, using my ability didn't affect my body, there was no cool-down to my ability. There was no opening in my ability for the enemy. But the problem was, I didn't know how to use it. After 2 weeks after I fell, I only understood my ability to absorb the energy around my body.

I was dejected to learn this because if I absorbed the energy from my surroundings, I might take the energy from the grass under my feet or animals, which might affect them. In the case of small plants, they would be killed by me, without any reason.

But when I experimented on it, I was wrong. It took me a whole day to understand how my ability absorbs. If I focus on my hands, my hand's skin will start to absorb and glow automatically, the more I focus, the more my hand glows.

The more it glows the more it gathers energy, and to release that energy I would have to punch something or use that energy. I placed my right hand on the grass and started to concentrate. At last, when my hand started to glow I removed my hand and saw the grass, it was still present and as green as ever.

So I summed up all things and finally concluded that my ability takes energy from the atmosphere. And I read in a book that 'or atmosphere has unlimited energy, the energy created by the god'. I was at the 9th sky after I learned it, I thought, 'I can use the power that the god himself creates.'

And then I started to have more and more experiments with myself as I marched towards the Magica.

While I was on the cloud 9 there were goblins marching for the villages. Their main motive was to attack the area, their attack would make people fear them and the people of Raisens and Elfins would move from the border. If these people shift, there won't be anyone to see their movements in upcoming years, thus increasing their chances of surprise attack.

CHAPTER TWENTY-FOUR

THE SAFEST BANK!!!

'It had been a month since I left the capital, she must be coming'.

Sometimes we only need hope to keep moving and sometimes even if we have all universe we still don't move.

****

"Sir Golo-Golo, it would take us another 1 week to reach the villages."

"hmmmmmm keep moving, you stinky green cockroaches." The goblin shouted and commanded all the rest 498 goblins,

"keep moving with your legs, says Sir Golo-Golo." Repeated the goblins.

On the day before the attack of the goblins, I finally reached the Magica; the safest bank. From the outside, it looked just like a stone castle, built with creativity. There was not a single window on the whole wall of Magica, except the ones at a great height.

At the gate, I witnessed the magical knights of Magica, these knights were created with magic, inside their complete body armor, there was no flesh. These knights are created by the Dwarves of Alnor. The 2 knights at the door held huge metallic spears. As I tried to walk in the guards drew their spears at me. I moved back, and as I moved back, they took their positions again.

At the gate, I met a dwarf named Tim. Tim was typically standing no taller than four feet tall but he had stocky builds and strong muscles. He wore a fine-built armor made up of steel. He did have a very long beard. He asked me who I was. I told him that I was Tyler Stark of the house Stark and was there to claim my property.

In response, he giggled and said, "Stark, you say, he is under the custody of King Jon and he won't let him run away."

I showed him the neckwear I had and the ring as well. He kneeled on his knees and said, "I am sorry lord Stark, I must not have giggled at your words, I am truly sorry for that."

"Well, it's okay, I didn't get dejected or anything and please raise your head," I told him.

"It has been always the same, all the Starks are as polite as ever," Tim said.

"And now there is only one," I said.

He lowered his head as if he must not have mentioned that.

I asked him, who he was and if he could help me, to get in.

He said that he is the in charge of sector 779-804 and also the in charge of giving people the interests." He added, "My father and grandfather and their grandfathers were loyal to your father and ancestors, so shall I will as well, I got a letter from the king to add all your wealth to his but in this process, he must prove that either you are dead or or or or."

"Or what Mr. Tim?" I asked.

"Well, I forgot the rule. It must be in the personal notes that I have made."

That was the moment I doubted him but in a book, I read about the dwarves that were loyal to us; loyal to the Starks. He showed his armor to the knights, and then they opened the huge steel gate for us. As we entered, I witnessed 11 dwarves at the reception. And around a hundred dwarves moving here and there. I noticed that some of the dwarfs were in armor and some were not, so I asked him about the wearing.

He said, "Sir, we dwarf are classified by what job we do here. For instance, look at me, I wear fine-made armor because I work deep down in the sectors, while if you look at the ones at the reception- they just wear fine cotton-made cloth. I am also the defender of the Magica, therefore I wear armor."

Furthermore, he added, "Once we reach my father, he will explain to you all things; as I am bad at explaining things. But you still have time left." Then he started to move towards a closed room, to the right side of the reception area.

I looked at the entrance gate, from where I just entered. 'shall I go back?' I thought to myself but this thought blurred as I thought, 'I won't, I have to show them what I am.' And then I started to follow Tim. I was amazed after arriving at the doorstep of the room of his father. On the door, it was written Kevin on a metallic plate. The metallic plate was hung at the door.

Tim knocked on the door with 2 of his fingers. Someone from the insides replied in a hoarse voice, "Come in, whoever it is."

Tim entered first, and immediately responded, "Well, the person is not someone."

His father pointing at Tim said, "You are someone only, at least only to me."

His father, Sir Kevin was arranging his books in the bookshelf.

"I agree, father, but I didn't mean it for me when I said that......" said Tim.

His father asked him, "Then whom have you got with?"

"Someone special" Tim told his father.

"Some royal member of a royal family?" he asked suspiciously.

"Sort of, I guess," he said with a smirkless smile.

"Gutter out the things, or leave this room, I have got work to do." His father said violently.

I was waiting at the door, 'it had been long enough' I thought and entered the room.

"Well Father, here we have Lord Stark of the Raisens, with us." Said Tim with honor for me.

"Starks are, my bad, Stark is in the castle, not here," said his father in a taunting way.

"Well, I guess you are mistaken about it. You have got a real living only Stark at your doorstep. And now don't deny that I am not a Stark." I said in a taunting way too.

"Boy, Starks are kind unlike you, they are kind with their actions, and with words too," Kevin said.

"I guess you were the one who started dishonoring my house." I addressed him with an argument.

"My bad kid, sorry for my actions and please don't sentence me to death," Kevin said in a taunting way.

"I won't if you help me claim my property," I told him.

He said, "A Stark shows up from nowhere and wants to claim his property. Anyways it's yours only, but didn't you want to donate it the King Jon and the great kingdom...."

"No, I don't want to name my things to someone from the Raisens, or to your great kingdom." I interrupted him in between.

'The king must have told them that I was donating it to him and the kingdom, such an old geezer he is.' I thought.

"Your great kingdom, you say, isn't it yours as well?"

"I guess yes and I guess no," I answered.

"You choose your words cleverly just like an elf's," he responded with his hoarse voice and with cough voice.

"Are you alright Mister Kevin?" I asked him.

"You are pretending to be heartless, aren't you?" He asked me.

"I guess yes and I guess no," I answered.

"Why? Why my lord?"

"The only way to save yourself from heartbreak is to pretend that you don't have one," I replied.

Both father and sir widened their eyes and Kevin said, "True, true words."

He added, "Well if you don't want to donate your ancestral treasures. Follow me and I shall show you the path that leads to your treasures and demonstrate to you, the Magica."

"*Father, I would also like to join you,*" Tim asked.

"*Ok then, let's get going downstairs.*"

CHAPTER TWENTY-FIVE

THE HISTORY OF MAGICA

As we walked, he demonstrated to me the Magica, "The great and safest bank, of all time, was built around 990 years ago. The job of building the bank, was to assure people of the Raisens and the Elfins were given to the dwarves, us. This place is being used by most of the merchants, landlords, royal ministers, and even by the kings and the queens of Raisens and the Elfins. As you can see there are rooms for different sections, each family or house chooses its respective employee here. The employee works for that house with loyalty. That's the reason why I am helping you to claim your treasures, because I am loyal to the Starks not to anyone else. To ensure that there is no theft here, we have created sectors. These sectors are guarded all day and night by the magical knights. Now to reach your sector we must take a lift. Come my lord, let's take one."

Everything was normal until I took that lift, the corridor had a red carpet, stone walls, rooms, candle stands, portraits, and many more decorative objects. At the end of the corridor, there was a golden-painted steel lift. The lift had a properly functioning door, though the lift wasn't covered from all sides. The walls of the lifts were no more than 4.6 feet high. There was a silver handle at the center of the lift.

I asked him on which upper floor my sector was. But both the dwarves smirked at me.

The lift started to move downwards. After the level of the lift decreased I was able to witness a huge-gigantic cave. Before the cave was hidden below the lift but now it got dispersed all in front of my eyes.

I was shocked to see the open-spaced cave.

Kevin continued, "The things you saw up were only our office, but this is the real bank. As you can see this dark cave has been lit up with our magical Open-fire torches. Although there is not much light in here it's adequate to see things, If not clearly. This cave was dug by the dwarves 997 years ago. It took them 7 years to complete the process. This cave was dug round and cylindrical, of radius about 600m and 160m deep. There are about 50 floors in total. Your treasure is kept safe in sectors 771-783, one of the safest sectors. Although each sector is safest the 700 series has given extra safety. We are still expanding the area of our bank. To ensure security, we have thousands of magical knights and thousands of dwarves and we also have some powerful magical beasts, from the Forest of Fantasy, guarding the series 700. Your treasures are at 100m depth. Your treasures are kept in sector 771 to sector 783."

We reached the 100m depth, the lift stopped and so was my heartbeat for a second. Tim opened the gate and I followed them, there were several guards and dwarves doing chit-chatting. None of them asked about our identities, maybe that was because Kevin and Tim were not unknown to them unlike me.

After walking for about 400m from the center of the Magica, we finally reached sector 771. After reaching there I witnessed a very thick and heavy steel gate, on that steel gate there was a huge angry face of someone and a 7-faced serpent on the top of the gate. Although it was made up of steel it in some sort gave me a frightening goosebump, I almost swallowed my salvia.

Tim continued the demonstration, as we reached there, "The sectors 771 to 790 are combined into one mega sector. As you can see a 7-faced steel serpent on the top of the gate, we have a 7-faced serpent in there."

"Well I am not a specialist in snakes, how in the world would he let me in?" I asked them in distress.

"That is something even I don't know, I thought the Stark would know about it," Tim said.

His words almost got me into anger but then I heard Kevin say "The eyes on the faces of the serpent would look at the ring you have and allow you to move to your treasures."

THE STARK'S TREASURY!!!!

"Well, is it necessary to go in to get the claim over my treasury?" I asked Kevin.

"Absolutely no" he answered.

"Then, why are you both insisting on me to enter in?" I asked them.

"Well, we wanted you to see," Tim said.

"Not interested at all," I said firmly.

"What's your problem? You don't want to see your treasures but want to claim them. Why??"

asked Kevin to me.

After a pause of some seconds I replied, "I just don't care how many jewels and diamond coins I have, the thing is that I want to prove it to them, prove it to her......"

"Prove it to whom ???" asked Tim in between.

"None of our business." Said Kevin to Tim.

"Then let's get back and get your paper work done." He further added.

"And then What?" I asked them.

"Then we would ask you to leave our bank as soon as possible." Said Kevin firmly.

He further murmured to himself, "Boy, who wants to prove?"

I actually got dejected after hearing his murmuring about me. Always, I was a sensitive person, all I pleaded was love and endless love.

Though I wanted fights between me and that loved one, still I didn't want her to humiliate me.

I kept my words to myself and followed them, "Why do people end up being rude to me?" I thought.

After following them to Kevin's office he said that he would do his signature, and my signature wasn't needed at all. He further asked me to leave and slammed the door close. I was still at the door when he slammed the door at me. I felt disconsolate being there, but still, I paused there for some seconds. That might be because I didn't expect that Kevin would do such a thing to me.

CHAPTER TWENTY-SEVEN

THE THOUGHTS PART-1

After some minutes I left the bank with my head low and my face of dejection.

That day I took place in an inn that was near to the Magica, around 5km away. The inn was filled with both elves and the people of Raisens. That was the second day I saw an Elf; the first elf face that I saw was of the King of the Elfins. I immediately ordered some food for myself and after I finished it, I asked the owner to send 900ml of milk to my room just before when they closed their food department.

It was nighttime, and I was lying at the bed thinking about the griffins and phoenixes. "griffins are better than phoenixes, serpents are also great, but in a fight between.............

I guess Griffins would be on the top of the table. Griffins have always been on the top, though there are even more majestic creatures out in the Forest of Fantasy........................ the white lions might also be considered a suitable choice........................... griffins are the best but it doesn't matter at all, I don't think a griffin will make any relationship or bond with me."

After my thoughts I started to think about my power, "I can gather the godly energy and use it by gathering the nature's energy into my body parts. I can also be used as a white torch however; I might be a bad one because my ability requires high concentration to gather the energy and even more concentration to maintain it. I can gain and understand how it works................. that must be due to my 12 hours of daily training. And my sword, I am still clueless how to call it back to me after throwing it........................ only if there was someone to teach me how to use it, use my power, so I would have progressed more than this."

After this, I started to think about how I could use my powers, 'hmmmmmmm.... I can run faster than any average warrior or human, I can increase the strength of my limbs and other body parts, this also allows me to swing my sword faster and with more force: increased enough force to completely chop off the tree into 2 pieces in a single blow. And my powers actually look very flashy, it may scare my opponent. If analyzed properly my ability has no flaws, though, I don't know what caused those shockwaves from my body.'

****

"Found that brat!" asked the king angrily to one of his guards.

"N...nnnnnnnnnn......oooooooo.............no my sir." Replied the guard with fear in his voice.

"Call my brother immediately." Ordered the king.

After some minutes the king's brother entered into the study: "Yes brother I am here, what do you want from me?"

"Get that stark kid alive or dead...." the king was continuing his sentence but was interfered with by his brother. "bro....."

"I don't care." Interfered the king in between.

"You should care." Said the royal king guard-king's brother.

"NO! Not for him." Said the king with a denying face. "Then I am sorry if you want me to participate in child killing, then I won't like to participate." Said the brother with all of his pride and honor.

"Even if I command you, anyways you may leave, I have a great surprise for you, a surprise that will blow your mind."

CHAPTER TWENTY-EIGHT

THE THOUGHTS PART-2

"I guess she overreacted to my proposal, maybe she is the reason why I am suffering here! I must not think like this about her, if I do I might end up cursing her with my words; I like her!.......... I LOVE her. It was my mistake, after all, I am too sensitive to be in this world, even if she was in anger and even if she asked me to leave, I mustn't have left, I should have stayed there and kept on asking her: I even don't know the reason why I am not suitable for her.................. I should have stayed there and not have left the place ...."

My thoughts got disrupted in between by a knock at the door.

"Who's it?" I shouted to respond to the knock at the door.

"Open the Door! little boy." said a strange voice from outside the door.

"I am Ronnie, the future owner of this inn, where do I put your 1L milk?" said the son of the current owner of this inn.

"Ronnie, sorry for being rude, please leave it at the console table, which is placed outside the room, and yes I wanted to say something to you................ I forgot I guess that was........Good Night." I said, in a gentle voice, to him.

"Good Night, Lord Stark." And he left the milk at the console table.

As I heard him go, I drew my body up from the bed, opened the door, and took the glass of milk inside the room.

I didn't want him to see my, hangdog looks at my face.

It seems when a person is depressed he tends to make other people around him feel okay rather than making them depressed as well. It was my problem that I was hated, but I never wanted to harm anyone's feelings. As I sat on the chair with a glass of milk in my left hand, a thought came to my brain, "As I had been marching through the inns, in the forest, I met people who were friends with each other- close friends I should say. They were very frank with each other; they abused each other, fought with each other and stayed with each other. I want that too, but back then if I had not been so sensitive I might have friends too. Why am I being so sensitive............ what for .... That's because I want people and her to admire me with all of their heart and soul, I want them to stick to me. I also want to be frank with them, want to do stupid things together. And I .... also want .... waannnttttt .... herrr ttooo ...... hold my hand, not anybody else's."

*****

"So what's there in your mind, why are you worried Ellena, my beloved daughter."

"*Nothing at all, Mom,*" *said Ellena with a sigh, as if she was worried.*

"*You know I am from the House Meadow; I know there is something you are worried of...........*"

"*Yeah, but I don't know, there is a very strange feeling, a feeling that I can't explain in words........*"

Her mother interrupted her in between and asked, "*You, in love?*"

"*Absolutely Not*" *replied Ellena immediately to her mom.*

"*Then what's it*" *asked the queen.*

"*A very strange feeling.*"

After some seconds, she continued, "*I don't know, but something feels odd, very odd.*"

"What's that something? My dear." asked her mom.

After some seconds, "As if something is going to happen, something wrong, very wrong........................."

"Or maybe something very good, something very right." Said her mom in an empathetic voice.

"Yes, maybe..." said Ellena as she stood up from her chair and stood next to the balcony.

She further said, "Yes everything's gonna be alright."

"Now this reminds me, would you like to go to the Forest of Fantasy? I talked to your teacher Jessica, she told me that you have nothing more to learn from her- now it totally depends on your practice. So would you like to go to the Forest of Fantasy?" Ellena's mom asked Ellena.

"Sure, why not, I would be delighted to go there, when can I leave for there?" said Ellena.

"You are full of energy, well you can leave, for the Forest of Fantasy, tomorrow; will you take someone with you."

"Hhhhhmmmmm.... Well no, I would go by myself." Replied Ellena.

"Hmmmmmm, I thought you would take Aaki, Daris, or your friend Isla with you." Said Ellena's mom with a smirking face.

"Don't feel anything wrong or suspicious, to me Aaki and Daris both are my brothers- for them as well I am their sister, Daris always calls me sister rather than taking my name......"

"And what about Aaki?" asked Ellena's mom.

"He is the same age as I am unlike Daris, who is a year younger. And Isla often regards me as her elder sister, and for me, she is a younger sister to me, though sometimes I have to guide her." Said Ellena.

Nobody knows from where her mother got this question. "Do you ever think of Tyler Stark?"

asked Ellena's mother to her.

"No Mom, never, whatever happened: it was the best possible way in which he would not get hurt. That was all I could do for him and for me as well, he surely hurt me, and yes he did. But now everything's fine for both of us, now he can actually move on easily."

"That brat..............."

Ellena interrupted in between and said, "In the first place I shouldn't have told you and secondly, you also are guilty, because you knew everything before I did." Said Ellena. "Yes I knew but I didn't expect him to do such reckless things. But now it can't be helped, he flew away and is nowhere to be found. He must have been a headache for you, a real......."

Ellena interrupted in between again and said, "Mom, I am feeling sleepy, I would like to get myself a nap, because from tomorrow my journey to the Forest of Fantasy will start."

"Okay then, Good night my little princess." Said her mother.

Her mom then moved out of Ellena's room, Ellena extinguished the candles with the blow of air from her air punch, and she then turned the fire torch off. She lay on the bed and murmured to herself, "Forest of Fantasy, I guess I would have to face Tyler."

****

On a mountain, all of the goblins were having their dinner: dog's flesh. These 500 goblins were there for almost 15 hours, planning their attack. "so here is the best possible plan, we would move from here and reach the middle town, which is 7km from the Magica........."

A goblin interrupted in between and said, "Golo-Golo I won't be going anywhere from her............"

"if you weren't the only magician goblin we have here I would have teared your tongue out."

"May I continue sir?" asked the goblin

"Yes," said Golo-Golo.

"Now none of us will be moving from here."
135

"HOLY Green!!!!!" shouted Golo-Golo in anger.

CHAPTER TWENTY-NINE

THE THOUGHTS PART-3

"Tyler why don't we go to the mountain."

"Yeah, why not Ellena We surely should," I said.

We both moved out of our room. I was wearing a white silk shirt and black comfortable pants, my hair uncombed. Her long hair accentuates her natural beauty."

As we both were running in the corridor I stopped, I saw her, and I stared at her as if we had never met.

"What happened, Tyler?" she asked me, in a very melodic voice, as she came to me.

I nodded my head, tears started to fall from my eyes.

Ellena lifted her hands and placed both of them on my cheeks, her hands were softer than cotton, and her fingers moved across my eyes to wipe my tears off. She smiled and said, "You are always a crybaby." She further said in a very emphatic voice, "Let's not just run but walk together."

I nodded again, but this time in affirmation. And then she took off her hands and we started to walk again. she out of the blue held my hand and blushed as she looked into my eyes.

Surely it was my first time, holding hands with my Ellena.

"So, what are the plans for today, Tyler?"

"I don't have any, hmmmm I would stick to yours," I said.

"That's even better because I have plans for us. First, we would visit our place of love, at that mountain, where you proposed to me and then we can decide about our plans."

I was as clueless as ever, but for me, everything was right as I held hands with her. As we walked we talked about our likes and dislikes, we talked and talked.

"Tyler, what do you think about love."

"Well, love is the best thing: it is powerful enough to transform a wild creature into an obedient buddy. Though, to me, only unconditional love is best, we love our partners with all our soul and heart." I started to regret a little because I shouldn't have said 'We love our partners with all our soul and heart' It might not be Appropriate- I thought.

"Achaa," she said in such a manner as if she was blushing internally.

{Achaa is actually a word from the Hindi language, which means a polite okay.}

"Ellena......" I was in hesitation but still asked her, "Ellena...... is everything Okay."

"Yeah, absolutely fine."

Her words: made me feel okay.

"By the way, there is something very important I wanted to ask you, Tyler." She asked in a very serious voice.

"What is it? Ellena" I asked her, though I was quaking in my boots.

"The thing that I wanted to ask is, what would you like to eat- Ramen or soba?"

This was very unexpected to me. I answered, "Ramen tastes better. Let's have ramen once we get home, from the place of love."

"Then let's hit the ramen for the lunch."

"Yeah," I answered.

I was very satisfied and glad to hear her voice again. Maybe it was a dream which got broken when I woke up. And finally, we reached the place of love, that place had colorful flowers swaying in the breeze, and the air was filled with sweet fragrances.

We both sat under the shades of the tree, it felt full of the joys of spring.

"Ellena, there is something I wanted to confess to you- I........"

"You are making the same mistake, again." She said to me.

All of a sudden I started to feel immense fear; the shiny weather, now changed to dark cloudy weather: Nimbostratus clouds covered the sky in a dark grey layer.

"I thought of you as a family, not like a future better half. I thought you changed, but nothing changed."

I couldn't say anything to her. I wanted to, but I was too scared. The weather got darker and darker until I was unable to see anything, then I heard a very rough voice 'Leave the place at once, you, brat of Stark.' The voice got louder and louder.

I screamed in fear and the words stopped, I was panting heavily and started to run as fast as I could. After some moments, I lost my breath and stopped to take one, just after I stopped: I started to fall downward and then a new strange voice said "Wake up...... wake up Lord Stark."

I immediately stood up and went back into the inn.

CHAPTER THIRTY

THE EXECUTION PART-1

"Wake up my dear."

"What is it, Mom?"

"Huh...... have your breakfast"

"But I guess it's still nighttime."

"Yeah, but soon enough the sun will rise; today I want you to pray with me to the God of Light-Sun."

"Achaa" said Ellena to her Mother.

"Come on now, let's have our breakfast, or else it would get cold."

After they both had their breakfast, the queen took her daughter to the balcony of the room, and they both prayed to god for his blessings.

After the prayer, her mother asked her if she remembered that she told her that she had a surprise for her. In response, Ellena nodded her head in affirmative and said, "I remember each and everything you have ever told me."

"Hmmmm... then you do have a sharp memory." Said her mother to her.

"Won't you ask me what it is?" asked her mother.

"Oh yeah. Mom, I was really eager to know my present. Please open up the locks to me." said Ellena with a very polite and emphatic voice- so as to ensure that her mother doesn't get hurt. She was actually a perfect person: though she forgot that she was being given a surprise she still insisted that she was eager to know about it.

"I won't tell you rather I would show you. Get ready and have a bath, your father is holding court in about 2 hours from now. I would like us both to be present there." Said her mother.

"Huh.... okay then."

The queen started to move out of the door but stopped and said to Ellena, "And yeah, wear elegant clothes today." And then she closed the door.

"What could the surprise be?"

****

"Everyone's heads here, the plan is that 250 of us would attack the village which is about 6km from the Magica. And rest 250 and I will be waiting here for your success and we will come for your help if necessary. And if we are still good to go we would attack the Magica as well. Let's wait till evening now- when the sun will be about to set off............... And someone gets me the meat" roared Golo-Golo.

****

Ellena was then 12 years old and I was 11 years-by age. The difference between our ages was exactly a year and 20 days.

"What do I wear............. elegant clothes: my mom said," murmured Ellena.

After Ellena got dressed elegantly, from her normal royal clothes, she headed towards the queen's room. "So you have come, my dear?" Said Queen Jenny.

"Yes... I guess I have arrived." Said Ellena.

"Then let's move to the court: it would be starting soon." Said Ellena's mom.

"Mom I am eager to know what surprise you have for me," said Ellena to her mother.

"I am eager too." Said her mother.

Her mother took her to the court. At the court, were the common people of Raisens and all ministers along with King Jon and his brother. The queen and Ellena sat on the chairs alongside the king and his brother. The king sat on the middle chair and on one side was his brother and on the other were Queen Jenny and her daughter. There was a table ahead of them, a long table that had, paper, feathers, and ink, on it. Firstly, Ellena sat on the cornermost chair, and then her mother on the chair beside her. The king was seated already and later his brother as well. the ministers were all standing in front of them with the common people.

The king started the court and said, "Before listening to your problems, I would ask you all to be silent for 5 minutes."

****

When I opened my eyes I was back in the inn. Just after I got my senses back I immediately stood up, the moment my brain reacted to its surroundings- an image of Ellena came in front of my eyes.

"Lord Stark, pardon me for disturbing you but the breakfast time is about to get over in 30 minutes. I hope you understand my conscience." Said Ronnie.

I was panting a little and not to mention I was all in sweat even though, I wasn't wearing anything.

"I understand you, Ronnie, I will be there in 10 minutes," I said.

"Okay, no problem." He said and left the room.

'What was that, I was with Ellena and then the weather turned all black. Did I hold hands with her and walk down the streets of Raisens?' It felt as if a dream had come true and soon I realized I was dreaming and started to cry

silently.

****

"Okay now let's pray to the god Vishnu," said the brother of the king.

All people present there joined their hands together and Prayed to the god. "Let's start the court now," said the king.

"My lord, with all of my respect I would like you to listen to the farmer George." Said a minister who wore a black plain cloak. An old aged person came forward and lowered his body a little in respect and said, "My lord, I came from a faraway village from the North-west. I saw some green goblins there...."

Everyone was surprised to hear that, and the brother of the king asked him "How many, did you see?"

"I didn't see, but my grandson did, he says he saw around 480." Said the old farmer George.

"Huh? And where is your grandson, Sir." asked the king's brother.

"He is not here, my lord."

"My dear brother, you yourself go with your men and see to it." Said the king Jon.

And he continued, "George, your grandson has done a great job out there. You should rest assured of the security of your village."

"Thank you, your majesty."

After listening to some more ministers, who were in the crowd, the king received a letter. As the problems got solved those people were allowed to leave the court. The king immediately unsealed it and read it and got furious.

The letter said

"To our king, the king of Raisens."

It is to inform you that the Stark boy appeared today, he has taken his treasures. He has no will to donate his precious items to the kingdom. I myself heard him talking with Sir Kevin and his son Tim. Sir Kevin asked him if he wished to donate it but he refused the advice. He has left the premises today only.

Yours Truly

Gourd

The king then passed the letter to the queen, to read. Ellena read it too along with the queen.

"Looks like I have got a reason to kill that brat." Said the king in a raged and frustrated voice.

Nobody dared to ask the king the reason for his anger and rage face.

The king said, "There is someone who has defied us, he has gone afar from us. He had taken the treasures of Raisens, from the

Raisens. Such acts of his are labeled as that of a traitor. I assure you all, that this person will be taken under custody and would be punished severely."

"Who is that bastard person, my king?" asked a minister who wore a green cloak.

"Tyler, Stark"

After hearing my name, the whole court felt a cold breeze of silence.

"Ssssss... Stark, I beg your pardon my grace." Said the minister in fear

"Why are you asking for pardon?" asked the king.

My king, he is Lord Stark." Responded the minister in a cracking voice.

"Why are you asking for pardon?" asked the king again. He further asked, "Who, he is now?"

"A Traitor, my King." Said the minister.

"I am giving a legal order, I command my beloved brother to go and hunt for him until he finds him. Bring him back here alive; if the boy uses any tricks to escape, he may use whatever way he pleads to capture him." Ordered the king Jon.

"My dear brother, May I ask a question to you?"

"Why not, move ahead." Said the king.

"What do you wish to do with him after I capture him for you?" asked the king's brother to the king.

"I already told you this once, but to make sure I will repeat myself: after his capture, that brat should be taught lessons of loyalty, he will be punished severely, as I mentioned already, he will face the repercussions of his sins."

"What sins, he has done?"

"Isn't it a crime to leave the palace without my permission or isn't it a crime to take the kingdom's money away from the kingdom I am damn sure that he must have done some more stuff that currently even we don't know." Said the king.

"What kind of teachings and punishments will he receive for his sins, my big brother?"

The king started to laugh heavily and said, "The worst ones, he won't receive actual teaching but some strikes of whips and some other punishments."

"Brother, let me remind you; you are going too far."

"That's what happens when someone breaks our trust." Said the king.

He further declared that he wouldn't listen to anything more.

"Everyone can leave!" shouted the king's brother.

And then everybody left the court; the only ones who remained were: Ellena, Queen Jenny, King Jon, and his brother.

"You are going too far, my brother or is it that you just want to look cruel in order to maintain peace in the court and fear amongst the ministers." Asked the

"That is up to you to think. My apologies to you brother but this time his punishment is going to be full of pain. We would at least give him adequate pain so that he does not defy us again. Adequate pain so that he survives and lives, but I don't think he would be able to live the same anymore."

"Are you going to make him a cripple, for life?"

"Good idea, why didn't come to mind? Thank you but I won't do that, he will be suffering immense pain that would make him a cripple." Said the king.

The king further added, "Now you may leave to capture him and kill the goblins as well."

"Yes. My king" said his brother.

Both the king and his brother left the court.

"Ellena don't get disheartened. He is just going to face the repercussions, of what he did." Said Queen Jenny.

"Huh? Achaaa"

****

After I stopped panting I forced myself to move up from the bed. As I stood up on my feet- I fell. I fell on the floor. My body was feeling very heavy, especially my chest region and there was a strange feeling in my stomach. My everybody part was filled with grief; my body wouldn't move even after I forced it to stand up. My fingers started to shake as I started to move them.

156

To be continued.......